# Skimmer & Birdy

## Let's Help Nell

Written By
Carrie Turley

Illustrated By
Ryan Law

For my dancing, singing, crafting,
fun-loving friend, Birdy.
- Skimmer -


For the lady whose heart was bigger than her
love of elephants. Miss you Mom.
- Ryan -

Skimmer and Birdy
ran through the grass,
feeling it tickle their toes.

They picked purple flowers
and twirled around,
letting the sun warm their nose.

They jumped in the air
and spread their arms wide,
grinning from ear to ear.

TRA-LA-LA

They sang, "tra-la-la,"
as they danced through the field
and gave each other a cheer.

They saw their friend Nell
walking tall through the field -
her head reaching up to the sky.
Her long skinny neck
swayed this way and that
as she held her head up so high.

Her cheeks and her nose

were scrunched up

on her face,

making her look very silly.

Her eyes
were shut tight,
she was biting
her lip,

and her feet

stepped along

willy-nilly.

Skimmer and Birdy
giggled and laughed
when Nell hit her head
on the tree.

They thought
she was teasing
and goofing around
until she fell down
on her knees.

They watched as she scrambled to get on her feet.
She puffed out her chest, looking proud.
But they saw the tear as it rolled down her cheek
and her smile that was hiding her frown.

They turned on their thinkers
and thought long and hard.

They puzzled
and wondered all day.

When the moon
and the stars
floated over their head,
they still
had nothing to say.

They tossed, and they turned
as they slept through the night,
dreaming of what they could do.

When morning came,
they both woke with a smile.
They had a plan - they knew!

They jumped
up and down.

They wiggled
and shouted.

They gave
each other
high fives.

Then it was time
to put their plan
into action.

They ran off
to gather supplies.

Skimmer grabbed bunches of leaves with her trunk. She spread them out flat on the ground.

Birdy picked clusters of beautiful flowers, collecting each color she found.

They crafted, created, and stitched them together, making a wide-brimmed hat.

Complete with two holes for Nell's pointy ears and some long stringy grass for a strap.

Just as they finished,
they heard a commotion
and saw Nell stumbling along.

They scooped up the hat
and ducked out of sight,
whistling Blue Bird's song.

Blue Bird came at once.
He landed before them,
dropping a worm
from his beak.

They whispered their plan
to their tiny blue friend
and asked him to help
them sneak.

He tweeted
and twittered.
He flapped his wings-
excited to help
his friends.

He scooped
up the hat
and flew
into the sky,

hovering
over
Nell's head.

Skimmer and Birdy
gave him a wink,
waving their trunks
in the air.

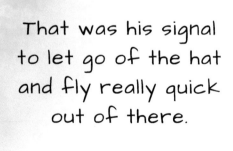

That was his signal
to let go of the hat
and fly really quick
out of there.

The hat fluttered down,

landing

square on Nell's head.

She stopped in her tracks,
looking stunned.

The colorful brim shaded her face,
blocking the light from the sun.

She opened her eyes
and untwisted
her face -

her
mouth
spreading
into
a
smile.

Without the bright sun
blinding her vision,
she could now see for miles.

She looked into the pond and found her reflection
staring back with a beautiful hat.

She twisted around looking for clues,
turning first this way - then that.

But Skimmer and Birdy
were clever and sharp.
They made sure
they couldn't be seen.

And Blue Bird sat snug
in his nest in the tree,
hidden behind leaves of green.

Nell shrugged her shoulders
and trotted away -
the smile
never
leaving
her face.

She didn't bump into
any more trees,
or fall, or get stuck
in one place.

Skimmer and Birdy gave Blue Bird a wave
and danced down the hill to play.

They picked purple flowers and twirled around;
happy they'd saved the day.

Nell didn't know who made her the hat.
She asked all her friends if they knew.
They shrugged their shoulders and looked confused,
never
suspecting
the two.

Blue Bird didn't tell.
Their secret was safe.

He flew away, whistling a tune.

Skimmer and Birdy
grinned when she asked
but never revealed the truth.

They sang, "tra-la-la,"
as they twirled in the sun;
their hearts feeling happy and bright.
Secretly acting in kindness and love
made helping their friend a delight.

Ryan Law loves animated movies/tv shows, video games, and drinking soda. He is a kid at heart with a big imagination. He prefers drawing cartoons because they have no limits and can make you feel all the feels.

Carrie Turley loves to put her "Thinker" on and write fun children's stories. Her favorite color is the rainbow, she sings off-key, and is happy to spend the afternoon solving problems with crafts. She is co-owner of Lawley Publishing, a children's book publishing company that focuses on clean, uplifting stories for children who believe in magic, have invisible friends, and will dance with elephants.

CPSIA information can be obtained
at www.ICGtesting.com
Printed in the USA
LVHW072121270521
688752LV00006B/41

* 9 7 8 1 9 5 2 2 0 9 3 2 1 *